Readers' Comments

When I started reading "The Marvelous Misfits
of Westminster", I found myself in a catch-22
situation: Should I devour the book or slow down
my reading pace so the story would last longer?
I just did not want it to end! I fell for the story
immediately.

Jasmin Borr (Amazon.de)

"The Marvelous Misfits of Westminster" is an
unexpectedly fabulous tale about a straight-laced
by-the-book dog show judge, who encounters an
extraordinary mutt [...]. The entertaining story captivates
the reader into suspending disbelief as it romps to its
satisfying conclusion.

MsRoux (Librarything.com)

A curious and delightfully well-written book about

a group of unlikely friends, lovers and their dogs.

KatoJustus (goodreads.com)

I felt a little in awe, as so much could be read into the

deeper meaning of the shadows that needed to be killed.

The characters were described beautifully. [...] Suitable for

all ages, "The Marvelous Misfits of Westminster" ticks

boxes for comedy, drama, and mystery, and definitely

covers all the feels!

Jacqui Corn-Uys (reedsy.com)

A small masterpiece [...]. I really haven't read

a short story so well written in a long time.

kimono_nero (lovelybooks.de)

Truly a bizarre story, but in a good way!

Katelynn (goodreads.com)

Want to Know More?

Are you interested in writing books and want to know how a book is created from idea to publication?

The process of creating *The Marvelous Misfits of Westminster* is documented on the author's website. Check it out on:

www.thestorytobe.com

The Marvelous Misfits of Westminster

A Story by

Andrea Hahnfeld

Cover-Design: Andrea Hahnfeld
Copyright Illustrations: canva.com (dog silhouette),
Andrew D. Taylor (paw prints)
Editing: Joel Pierson
Written and published with ulysses.app and Affinity Publisher
Text Copyright © Andrea Hahnfeld 2021
Augustenstr. 3
04317 Leipzig (Germany)
thestorytobe@gmail.com

This work including all its parts is protected by copyright. You may not copy, distribute, transmit, reproduce or otherwise make available this publication (or any part of it) in any form, or by any means. This applies in particular to reproductions, translations, microfilming and storage as well as processing in electronic systems. Any exploitation is prohibited without the prior written permission of the author.

E-Book: ISBN 978-3-949301-00-1
Paperback: ISBN 978-3-949301-01-8
Hardcover: ISBN 978-3-949301-07-0
Audio Book: ISBN 978-3-949301-02-5
Visit www.thestorytobe.com to find out more
about the author and this book.
All rights reserved.

To Chris

Today

The Hunts and I are parked at the shabby side of the center of the universe, a little away from her trailer. It took us a while to find the trailer park, as it doesn't appear on any map. The place looks desolate. There's junk everywhere. What isn't covered in garbage is overgrown with weeds. The air is hot and oppressive. Something's brewing. A storm, if we're lucky. Those storm clouds are unnerving me, though. They look not quite natural, as if someone had painted them—someone with a vicious sense of humor.

It's quiet. Too quiet. Even the strays are missing. No cats, no dogs. Apart from us, there's only a boy. He's sitting in the dust in front of a boarded-up trailer, pitching pebbles at a tin can.

"You sure she lives here?" I ask, though I know she does. Not only is it written in skin, but Irving sniffed her out too. Still, my heart refuses to believe. When she rejected any of my money ten years ago, I figured she had made other arrangements. Realizing she'd lived like this all those years tears my heart.

Through the rearview mirror, I look at Haimi in the back seat. Irving has curled up into a ball on her lap and is snoring softly.

"You want me to read it again?" Haimi asks. She knows I'm looking at her. How is a mystery to me. But she always does.

"Don't be silly, dear," Harvey says. "You've read it to him a hundred times." The coughing sound is him laughing. "Haven't I undressed enough already?" He pats my thigh to get my attention. As I look, he winks at me and points with two thumps at his skin.

I roll my eyes, but my mouth pulls into a smile. "I know, I know ... 'This skin ain't joking.'"

With a sigh, I get out of the car. Every fiber tells me to get her out of this place. But this is not my story. I'm just the sidekick helping the hero along. As I walk to the back of the car, I tug at my shirt. It clings to me like it's trying to hold me back. *Why on earth did she run away to hell?*

I open the trunk and get out the box. It's large and heavier than anticipated. I press it against my chest and walk carefully over to her trailer. At the doorstep, I bend my knees in a slow, fluid motion. The box clunks to the ground, despite my effort. I breathe in sharply and wait. Nothing. I peek through the air holes in the lid, but it's too dark inside to see anything. So, I put my ear on the box to double-check. With relief, I hear steady breaths and a low snore. I retie the bow, securing it with a double knot for good measure. Time to go. Before I leave, I stroke the lid and whisper, "You catch it, girl, and when you do, kill it. Kill it before it kills her!"

Four Months Ago

Thirty minutes after Cynthia has phoned me, I leave the icy winds of Eighth Avenue and enter The Garden through entrance C. The air inside the arena is heavy with the scent of wet dog, canned food, and ammonia. Excited barks and hectic voices fill the corridors. I am back where I belong. I straighten my bow tie, smooth my hair, and walk with my head held high through the crowd, looking for Cynthia.

Five years have passed since my last dog show. I did not expect to be a judge at Westminster ever again. Yet, I still make sure to look the part. Every year, just in case. Come Westminster weekend, I dress up in my tawny-brown three-piece suit, put on my best leather shoes, freshly shined, of course, and—to introduce a splash of color and a whiff of elegance—I wear my favorite bow tie. It's fern green and according to the person who gave it to me, it suits the color of my eyes.

Cynthia has begged me to step in. Nonetheless, I feel like an intruder. Even though I did the right thing back then. I defended Westminster's standards. My principles did not waver in the presence of a crowned head. Doing what's right cost me my job. The board had me canned for it. An injustice that still stings.

A couple of the more seasoned participants recognize me. With a nod, they step aside to let me pass. I nod back, warmth rushing through my chest. The board might not appreciate what I have done for Westminster, but who gives a fiddlestick about their opinion? I certainly don't.

"Clement!" Cynthia rushes toward me through the crowd, clipboard in hand. Her gray ensemble is loosely cut, her flat shoes of the obviously comfortable kind, her hair up in a messy bun. She looks just as I remember: not at all like a lady. She doesn't talk posh either. Not with me.

"Only sound travels faster," she says with a surprised look at her wristwatch, then greets me with a kiss on the cheek.

"Cynthia!" I kiss her back. "To what do I owe the unexpected honor?" The question is intended as a quip, but once my words hit the air, the bitter tone that has mixed in is undeniable.

Instantly, the atmosphere changes. Awkwardness spreads between us like spilled ink.

"I know our last encounter wasn't exactly pleasant." Cynthia stares at her clipboard, fidgeting with the ballpoint attached to it with a rubber band. A palpable silence stands between us like an invisible person.

"You were totally right. There are rules to be followed. Nobody should be allowed to enter finals directly. I did not approve of the board's decision. They should not have fired you in the first place. Yet, I thought if a friend told you what they'd decided, it would soften the blow." She looks up; in her eyes, a plea for forgiveness.

I *do* know she had merely been the messenger I'd shot at in my anger. I even could imagine she had stood up to the board on my behalf. Still, it feels good to hear her say it. I was canned for doing my job too well. That doesn't happen every day, and it still gnaws at my pride. All those years it was *my* sense of perfection that had kept up the standards of Westminster. After all, the show is an institution. It means something to win it—at least to me. I take a deep breath to push down my bitterness. None of us can change what has happened. Cynthia and I had been friends once. She still wants to be mine.

"How can I be of service, milady?" I ask, hinting at a bow.

Cynthia purses her lips, but her eyes twinkle. I can tell she takes my mild mockery of her position for what it is: a peace offering.

"I should never have told you this."

"You didn't," I say, smiling.

I'd found out what kind of family Cynthia came from years ago during a visit to the Old World. She was not amused by our chance meeting at Balmoral Castle. I was discussing one of the queen's corgis with a footman who referred to himself as *Doggie One*, a lordly schmuck. Her Majesty contemplated showing the dog at Westminster—without competing in the preliminaries. Though *Doggie One* did his utmost not to utter any request along those lines, it was obvious he tried to achieve a mutual understanding. The corgi's name was Willow, a real cutie but no show winner—although I kept this opinion to myself. Her Majesty's wish certainly wasn't my command. No way I'd let her dog skip to the finals.

I was in the process of breaking the news to His Royal Schmuckness, when up the garden stairs walked a familiar figure dressed in very unfamiliar attire. The woman walking next to the Prince of Wales wore a Balmoral tartan, combined with an expensive riding jacket in traditional brown tweed. The rough winds of the Highlands had ruffled her hair and reddened her cheeks. Cynthia nearly fell out of her muddy rain boots when she recognized me.

Back in New York, I never told anybody about our chance encounter in Scotland. Clearly, Cynthia had moved to America to be someone else. She appreciated my discretion. We became friends thereafter.

I expect more banter, but Cynthia says no more. Instead, she bites her lip, eyeing the room behind my back as if looking for someone.

"What's up?" I touch her arm to get her attention.

"Have you been following the show?" she asks, pinching the skin at her throat.

I shake my head. Since my forced retirement, I avoid watching any live broadcasts. It hurts too much. Usually, I read the *New York Times* coverage a few weeks after. Cynthia nods. "I figured." She takes my arm and pulls me to a quiet place near the wall.

"There has been an unusual decision during the Best of Group event yesterday. An unacceptable one, to be honest. I'm not talking about slight imperfections here. The members of the board are upset." A mischievous glint flashes in her eye. "Truth is, they lost their shit. Pardon my French."

"I'm the cavalry then?"

Cynthia nods. She is all serious again. "This could be your way back to Westminster. They want *you* to judge the Best in Show event. The board knows you'd rather drop dead than turn a blind eye to even the slightest imperfection."

"As would you," I say.

"Well, to be honest, I *was* their first choice. But I excused myself for personal reasons."

I furrow my brow. "I find it hard to believe that any judge at Westminster would make an unacceptable judgment. Each one of us has years of experience. Who'd do such a thing?"

Cynthia presses her lips together and stares intently at her clipboard as if trying to find the answer to my question there.

"Spit it out. What haven't you told me?"

"It was Edith."

Every muscle in my body tenses as if punched. I haven't seen Edith in years. Since she disappeared, she's gone to lengths to avoid running into me. Even excused herself as a judge from shows I was hired to judge too. Her memory haunts me like a murdered person's ghost, but despite that, the mere possibility of a chance meeting doesn't even cross my mind anymore. I put my trembling hand into the pocket of my jacket.

"Will you still judge tonight?" Cynthia avoids my gaze. She knows exactly what she's done. Of course, Cynthia hasn't told Edith I am coming either. She can't afford to lose a judge in the middle of the event. She has thrown both of us into the deep end.

I breathe steadily through clenched teeth, counting to ten in my mind before I answer. "Of course. I just need a moment."

Cynthia nods and squeezes my arm. "I'm truly sorry. I owe you one. Big time."

Without another word, I turn and hurry to the washroom. The cold water I splash on my face is a relief. I study my face in the mirror. Since Edith left, it has turned into a web of worry and pain. What will she think of me after all these years? Has it been ten already? To occupy my trembling hands, I adjust my bow. I take a deep breath and straighten my shoulders. It can't be helped. Besides, why should I care what she might think of me? My turning into a bitter old man is her doing. She owes me an explanation—

and today I will get it. With renewed determination, I leave the washroom.

Preparations are in full swing, as the show is to start in less than one hour. People are brushing and blow-drying their dogs on both ends at the same time. All grooming tables are crowded. All but one. Curious. Is one owner late? I walk to the abandoned workstation and right into the olfactory wall that surrounds it. I wrinkle my nose. The scent is earthy. Earthy with a hint of bad wolf. I can't shake the feeling of having ventured too deep into the woods. The very next moment, a black beast jumps at me out of nowhere, teeth bared. The claws of its plate-sized paws dig into my chest, and its deep growl makes me freeze. I dare not move and avoid looking at it, in order not to provoke it any further.

"Irving, that's no way to greet a guest!" a fine voice says, rebuking the dog good-naturedly.

An eerie silence spreads from the dog that hushes all other noises. For a split second, only the beast and I exist. When the sounds return in a deafening wave, they almost drown out the fine voice that says, "I see. In this case, good catch. But still, not quite the way to gain a friend."

A wrinkled hand pulls at the dog's leather band, which is way too delicate to hold back a hound of Irving's size. Before the dog lets go of me, it runs its slobbery tongue across my face.

With the body of the beast out of my view, I see who is talking, an elderly lady wearing a brown felt hat with a wide brim and a dress in at least a dozen shades of green. She is tiny in relation to her dog.

"That's better, Irving. A kiss reconciles everyone." She giggles.

Boiling with rage, I wipe the drool off my cheek with the back of my hand. "Good catch? What's that supposed to mean?" The woman opens her mouth to say something, but I cut her off. "You do know, ma'am, that it is against the rules to bring a dog to the event if it does not compete in it?"

Indignantly, I glare at the black monstrosity that now sits meekly next to its owner, nestling its calf-like head to her hand. Its eyes, though, never leave me for a second. They have the peculiar shade of the ocean. One is tempted to perceive them as a lovely blue, but truly they have no color of their own. They merely reflect something else.

"I don't understand ..."

The old woman lifts her head and gazes at someone standing right behind me. Her eyes are misty, like November fog. Did I just rebuke a blind woman and her guide dog? My ears start to burn.

"I am so sorry, ma'am! I didn't know ..." I stammer.

The woman laughs good-naturedly. "You are not the only one. Irving may not look like a typical show dog, but believe me, he is a true Eppinger." She lovingly plucks the dog's left ear, which hangs limply down while the right one stands straight up. The one sticking up is missing a big piece.

I open my mouth to say something, then close it again. No string of words expresses my bewilderment at her statement in quite the right way. Among all the confusing things contained in that sentence, I first tackle the one that hurt my professional pride.

"As a longtime member of the American Kennel Club and seasoned judge at Westminster, I can assure you a breed named Eppinger does not exist," I say.

"I thought so too." The woman smiles. "Then I met Irving."

I rub at my brow, wondering who's let this crazy person in. "Westminster is a breed event. Surely, you are aware, ma'am, that a single dog does not make a breed. He cannot compete."

"Eppingers are quite rare, and Irving's one of a kind, but he is not the only one. There's another Eppinger in the show today."

I shake my head. "I mean no disrespect, but to compete in today's event, a dog must have won the prelimi—" She puts a blue ribbon in front of my nose like a police officer flashing her badge.

I stare at the imprint. *Best Working Dog.*

It dawns on me whom I have met: Edith's infamous decision.

I look at the mongrel in front of me. Irving's the size of a full-grown Shetland pony. His coat is matted and dirty. Bald spots reveal his crusty skin. His pale tongue dangling limply from his mouth gives the impression of great exhaustion. It's hard to tell how old the dog is, but its prime years are long past. If one saw a dog like this roaming the streets, one would have pitied it enough to throw it a half-eaten hamburger. But I doubt anyone in their right mind would take it home with them. Although the ribbon in my hand is proof, I cannot wrap my head around the fact that Edith should be responsible for such an outrageous judgment. We used to have very similar ideas of what winners looked like. She must have changed a lot. *Or maybe you never knew her at all,* says a growling voice inside my head that is not my own.

"I ... I am sorry," I stammer and hand the blue ribbon back to her, "my mistake."

She smiles again. "An easy mistake to make. We are the only ones breeding Eppingers, and this is our first show."

I wonder where the name comes from. It has a familiar ring. *Isn't there a town named Epping in New Hampshire, on the crossroads of Route 101 and Route 125?*

"The breed's not named after Epping, the center of the universe, although this would be fitting," says a panting voice behind me, followed by the husky bark of a long-time smoker. "They are named after Epping, the forest near London."

"Excuse me?"

I turn, and a sharp yelp escapes my mouth. The person in front of me has no lips. Bared teeth stretch out toward me, and a thin thread of saliva drips from the open mouth. I do not know what I am looking at, a man or a woman. The clothing and the depth of the voice rather suggest a man. Where the ears should be, there is only a shriveled piece of skin resembling dried plums. A tuft of hair grows out of the skin halfway up the neck, as if the hairline has melted, coagulated, and solidified in the new place.

"I'm Harvey Hunt." The burned man sticks out his hand. I stare at it. Like every other patch of visible skin, the hand is scorched and scarred.

"If you are contemplating running, the time would be now," the man says. The burning sensation in my ears makes me remember my manners.

"I'm sorry. I didn't mean—" I take his hand. The grip of his handshake is firm, almost painful.

"Don't worry. I'm used to it. You don't see a scary face like this one every day." Harvey points with two thumbs at his face and winks at me. The strange hoarse sound comes out of his throat again. It takes me a while to realize it is a laugh.

"I see you've already met my wife, Haimi, and our little showstopper." He tousles Irving's shaggy hair.

I snort at the word *showstopper* but immediately camouflage it as a cough. Harvey looks at me intently.

"How *did* you know I was wondering about the breed name?" I ask to deflect from my involuntary reaction.

Harvey lets it pass and winks at me again. "I have my sources."

"So, are you from London, originally?" They do not sound very British to me.

Harvey shakes his head. "We are from Maine. But Irving's a true Brit. His ancestors lived in Epping Forest after they escaped the London Massacre." The burned man notices my empty gaze. "You know, the one in 1939 that killed almost 400,000 dogs?" I shrug. "Anyway, they were a legendary pack. Did all kinds of great things. Even saved fifty-one people from drowning the night the *Marchioness* sank on the River Thames. Great shame all but one got slain shortly after. They shot the dogs by the dozen. Can you believe it?"

I can't. I have never heard of any massacre in London or of any dogs getting shot by the dozen in Epping Forest. But I do know about the *Marchioness* disaster. Everyone my age knows. It had been all over the news in the eighties. The steamer was hired for a birthday party, and it had 130 people on board. It sank in the late eighties after it got hit twice by a dredger. The dredger's crew did not make any attempts to rescue survivors, and fifty-one people drowned. No dogs were involved at all. This conversation has turned into a hostage situation. I look at my watch, planning a polite escape from the couple who are as nutty as a fruitcake.

"At least one of the pack survived." Harvey sighs heavily and strokes the dog as if to comfort it.

Now, he has my attention again. Yes, the dog looks like he's ready to drop dead. But I doubt Irving is any older than twelve. "Sir," I say with furrowed brows, "the *Marchioness* sank more than thirty years ago."

"You tell me. I was on that boat. It was my birthday party." For a moment, he says no more but stares at his burnt hands. He takes a deep breath and nods at the dog. "That one dragged me out of the water. He dragged me out of other things too. I'm prone to accidents, you see." He makes a gesture including his whole body. "Maybe that's why Irving stayed with me and didn't return to the woods with the others. He knew I was not to be trusted around the elements." He twists his lipless mouth into something that probably counts for a smile. I do not know how to react, so I laugh nervously.

Irving pierces me with his aqua-colored eyes. The dog is gigantic by canine standards. But dragging a grown person out of a river? Against the heavy currents of the Thames? *Come on.*

"For what do you breed then?" I ask, suddenly curious.

"Extraordinary abilities," Haimi says.

I can't deny that I am intrigued by the notion. Irving's eyes continue to pierce me, and despite my doubts, I wonder what extraordinary ability the dog might have.

"Read thoughts, among other things," says Harvey as if it were a side note.

"So, he's the one?" Harvey has turned toward his wife and to the dog when he says it. But I am almost certain the question is directed at the dog alone. "That's what he says," replies Haimi, and the dog blinks twice.

Harvey looks me up and down. His gaze gets stuck on my bow tie. "Doesn't look like the helping kind to me."

Confused, I glance at the three misfits who are inspecting me as if I am some kind of mythical creature. Not of the helping kind, of course. My bow gets tighter the longer they stare at me. I pluck at it to get some air.

Haimi moves forward and grabs my hand. "Do you believe in transmigration?" she asks.

"Of the soul?" I ask.

Haimi does not answer but steps closer. I feel the warmth of her breath. "May I?" she asks. Not waiting for my consent, she slips my hand under Harvey's shirt and presses it onto his disfigured skin. I flinch, but Haimi holds me there with surprising strength.

"Close your eyes, so you can see!" she urges.

I'd rather keep my eyes open, but I am afraid she won't let go of my hand if I don't obey. Blindly, I grope my way over the scar tissue. Harvey's skin feels unexpectedly tender and soft, as if it might break under my touch. The scarred lines and elevations form a fascinating pattern. Almost with a mind of their own, my fingertips explore the structure, trying to decipher it like a foreign language. A higher power seems to guide my hand as it glides over the burned man's naked skin.

"The scars," Haimi whispers into my ear, "they are not random. They form a pattern. Feel here." She guides my hand to a scarred area near Harvey's left nipple, her voice now a hypnotic mumble. "That's about you. Well, not all of it. Those bumps over here are about some cricket. But this patch, that's about you. Shall I tell you what it says?"

Perhaps Mrs. Hunt interprets my silence as approval. More likely she doesn't even care if I want to know.

"I need you, Hal." She breathes the words into my ear.

I tear back my hand and glare at both. "Is this some kind of joke?"

Harvey shakes his head slowly, pushing his shirt back into his trousers. "This skin ain't joking," he says, wiping a drizzle of saliva from his mouth. "You are Hal." He does not look at me, but at the dog when he says it, waiting for its reaction. Irving blinks twice.

Before I can respond, a voice behind me draws my attention. With a stumbling heart, I turn and see Edith amid a group of other judges.

"He's something else," she says to a colleague walking next to her. But right when she utters those words, our eyes meet, and I feel as if the words are meant for me. She wears her brown hair short now, brushed back behind her ears, which gives her a boyish look. Her skin has lost the healthy glow I knew. It is pale, almost translucent. Dark circles have gathered around her eyes, making them unnaturally large. She couldn't have looked more like a ghost if she'd tried. What has happened to her between then and now? When she realizes whom she is facing, her radiant smile fades. She stares at me like a wild thing caught in a speeding car's headlights.

My last memory of Edith is an absence rather than a presence. The sound of her shower. The scent of her body wash. It smells like a meadow in spring. Behind the bathroom door, she hums. *The Moldau.* Edith's impression of the river passing the jubilant Hunters—a part usually played by the French horns—is charmingly out of tune. I smile. Edith has asked me to dress up. That means she wants to tell me something important. *Could it finally have happened?* I rummage in the fridge for a suitable drink.

Should I open a bottle of wine? I shake my head. If it *has* happened, that's hardly appropriate.

It takes me a while to notice the sudden silence. The water's still running. But her humming has stopped. The apartment has turned as quiet as a forest without any birds.

"Cricket?" I knock softly on the bathroom door. "Everything all right?"

No answer. I enter and find the steamy room empty. Turning the water off, I look for Edith in the adjacent bedroom. I do not find her there, nor in the rest of the apartment. She has disappeared. All I find is the empty package of a pregnancy test.

A week later, she served me with divorce papers. The whole thing went through her lawyer. I never saw or spoke to her again. Losing her was abrupt and permanent. As if she had died.

"Isn't it a remarkable breed?" She kneels beside Irving and pats the dog's unshapely head. Some judges inspect the tips of their shoes, others bite their lips. Edith does not notice. The dog entrances her. I recognize that gleam in her eyes. She wore it when she said "I love you" the first time. My insides turn cold in a fit of unreasonable jealousy. I won't name this abomination Best in Show—not for all the tea in China.

The group of judges moves on. When Edith gets up to follow them, Irving snatches her forearm and holds her tight. Tight enough to hurt, but not to break the skin. Clearly the dog does not intend to let go of her. Edith freezes. She knows how to act around dogs. Nonetheless, her hand trembles.

The other judges have stopped mid-step and look at the scene, horrified. I move forward, intending to grab the dog and tear it away from her. But Harvey holds me back.

"No, let him have a good bite first. Don't you see how close it is? It needs a good scare!" he urges.

"What are you talking about? Let go of me. This is madness." I shake off his hand. But something in Edith's eyes holds me back. She's not afraid of the dog. She does not look at her arm but fixates on what the dog has caught. Her eyes are wide with wonder. I can't see anything, but she obviously does. As does the dog. And Harvey.

With cautious steps, the burned man approaches Edith and Irving. He bends down to the dog.

A minute passes in tense silence. The dog and owner lock eyes. Both drool.

When Harvey's voice breaks the silence, it comes from afar and sounds unlike his own. Almost like a growl. "The shadow comes with the child. It has killed before. It will kill again. Do you understand?"

Edith's face blanches with fear. She holds my gaze, unable to blink, and her chin quivers. Almost imperceptibly, she nods. Irving lets go of her immediately, licks Harvey's hand as if to thank him, and sits down in front of Edith, staring at her. His eyes appear almost black now, as if reflecting a darkness. Edith rubs Irving's drool off her arm.

"I'm fine," she says and holds her arm up, so everyone can see she isn't hurt. "Just got a fright. Please go on without me." Her voice trembles. I see that she struggles to hold back the tears.

The crowd stands rooted, shocked, not sure what to do.

"This dog should wear a muzzle. Better yet, be disqualified," says one.

Another mumbles, "What has Westminster become? A gypsy circus?"

"Not if I have a say in it," I say and shoo the bystanders away as if securing a crime scene. Edith needs some space, and I need room to think. *The shadow comes with the child.* Harvey's words have meant something to her, as had the names Cricket and Hal to me. A hot wave rushes through my veins and quickens my pulse. Is there a child? I remember the empty box of the pregnancy test the night she disappeared. I'd assumed it had been negative. I look at Edith intently, but she avoids my gaze.

"You'd better keep your revelations to yourself, Mr. Hunt." Her voice sounds unaffected, but her body betrays that she is shaken. She has her arms crossed in a peculiar self-hug to hide the trembling. Then her eyes fall on Irving. "Perhaps I was wrong after all. There is nothing special about this ... mutt."

She turns around and practically runs away. I am left alone with the Hunts and their dog.

"She needed to know. The shadow already left its marks on her soul. Her death is inevitable if she does not get help. *Your* help." With her bony finger, Haimi circles the spot on Harvey's chest she has shown to me.

"It's written in fire. She needs you, Hal. *We* need you. Irving *must* win."

My body tenses up, and my muscles start to quiver. It takes some self-control not to shout at the elderly couple in front of me. "No sane person would ever name this dog winner of anything."

Haimi's cheeks turn red as if slapped. "Sanity, dear friend, needs to be handled with extreme caution. Do not let it prevent you from stepping through a wall just because you won't believe it to be a door."

The old lady's chest moves violently up and down. Harvey touches her arm. His wife shrugs in silent agreement and says no more.

"Irving is dying," Harvey says. "He needs to procreate. With the other Eppinger in the show." He turns his head. I follow his gaze to Lady Winthrop's workstation. She is brushing her Salvatora.

I stroke my brow and take a deep breath. They are mad. Complete nutcases. "You. Cannot. Be. Serious," I say through gritted teeth, ignoring the obvious: the fact that Lady Winthrop's dog is not an Eppinger but a fox terrier. "What on earth makes you think she would ever let this mutt jump her prize-winning Salvatora? Lady Winthrop is known to be picky with mating choices. I assure you, the prize money will not be enough to convince her."

Harvey shrugs. "True. Money did not convince her. But like many a noblewoman, she couldn't resist a good bet. She agreed to a mating. On one condition—"

"Irving must win," I complete, my voice sounding exhausted. As I shake my head, I wonder what they have offered Lady Winthrop in return, to make the bet tempting enough for her to even consider it.

"Don't worry, it won't come to it." Harvey pulls back the corners of his lipless mouth to a dreadful smile. It makes his teeth stick out even more and causes a gush of spit to drool onto his shirt. Appalled, I avert my gaze. If he has noticed my disgust, he does not let it show. Instead, he continues with enthusiasm. Maybe he believes I finally understand what it is all about. "Now you see where you come in. I knew you would. It wasn't easy to get you here either. We had to ..."

He rambles on about an obscure scheme of Irving's that involved Edith. And Cynthia. And supposedly forced all the members of the board to change their mind about my being a judge at Westminster. I only listen to his baloney with half an ear while my mind rattles in an effort to come to terms with the mere notion that Lady Winthrop would ever agree to such a bet.

In mind-boggling disbelief, I watch her brush Salvatora with a passion. Even from a distance, I notice how shiny and healthy the dog's fur looks. The bitch is a rare kind of perfection: coat markings as if drawn by an artist's hand, eyes the color of golden syrup, impeccable posture, and a winning temperament. Salvatora exceeds all breed standards and is, in every aspect, an undisputed ten. Already, the smooth-haired fox terrier is a living legend. Salvatora has won Westminster three times in a row and is expected to win a fourth time today. If she does, that will be a feat no other dog has accomplished before her in the 147 years Westminster has existed.

"Now, just when you had me all convinced that looks don't matter in a true Eppinger," I say matter-of-factly, but the blind woman is not that easily fooled.

"It's not Salvatora's beauty that makes her special." Haimi's voice sounds rebuking. "She smells imminent peril. Salvatora comes from a long line of survivors. One of her ancestors survived the sinking of the *Titanic*."

Haimi takes my hand and presses it. She looks at me forcefully with her misty eyes.

"The connection between Salvatora and Irving is vital. Their offspring will save many lives. Edith will be one of them. You are destined to bring about their connection."

I shake off her hand. Finally, I have had enough of the Hunts' antics. "Or what?" I spit. "Edith dies? You're out of your minds." I glare at them. "If your plan is to scare me into helping you, count me out."

"As you will," says Harvey. He delivers the words like a line in a play. I can't shake the feeling he chose them with intent. But how would he know?

As I leave them to look for Edith, I can't get a word out of my head: *proof*.

Edith sits on the stairs leading to the loading area, her arms wrapped tightly around her knees. She is watching the play of shadows on the concrete floor and seems lost in thought. The place is deserted this time of day. Only a few empty boxes next to the trash cans and a parked truck betray the bustle of the morning hours. Apart from the emergency lighting, the area is dark. One of the lights flickers, giving the shadows around us a peculiar vividness.

Edith only notices me when the door falls shut. She looks up. "Hal…" She sniffles. The redness of her eyes betrays that she has been crying.

A warmth spreads through my body when she uses the pet name she'd given me in happier times. It hits me like a bullet of heat. Nobody else calls me by that name. It's our little inside joke.

For our first Christmas, she gave me a signed copy of Hal Clement's short story "Proof." My favorite story, by my favorite science fiction author. She knew I was a big fan of his. After I'd opened my present, I proposed to her on impulse. She'd agreed by quoting the last line of the story: "As you will." That made me love her even more.

She called me Hal ever since. I am glad she still does. All anger, all resentment falls away from me.

I sit down beside her. We are closer to each other than we have been in a long time. The warmth of her body makes me quiver. I hand her the handkerchief, which I carry in my breast pocket—always freshly washed and neatly folded—for occasions just like this. It has been a while since my chivalry was needed.

She accepts it, dabs her eyes, and then blows her nose vigorously. This makes me smile. The girl I have fallen for is still in there. Somewhere.

"Nice bow tie," she says. "Suits your eyes."

"So I'm told."

She smiles.

I stroke back a strand of her short hair that has fallen into her face. All of a sudden, the old intimacy between us is back.

"Tell me, Cricket," I say.

Edith begins to sob uncontrollably. It takes a long time before she's able to speak.

"I'm sorry, Hal. I was terrified." Her gaze is pinned to her lap. She wrings the handkerchief in her hands. They still tremble. I take them into mine to hold them steady, they are ice cold.

"Forget the Hunts. They are crazy."

She pulls her hands away and crosses her arms. She avoids my gaze and stares into a dark corner next to the trash cans instead. When she speaks again, her voice is so low, I can hardly hear her.

"It was me who found her."

By her toneless voice, I can tell she is referring to her mother. I've never met Margaret. She had killed herself when Edith was still a child. Edith rarely speaks about the circumstances of her mother's death. But when she does, her voice becomes hollow as a shell to hide the pain.

I sit there frozen, not knowing how to react.

"There was a letter," she says. "I didn't show it to anyone. Burned it right after reading. *The shadow comes with the child,* it said."

My thoughts are racing as fast as my pulse.

"When Margaret became pregnant with Edith, her parents forced her to marry me," my father-in-law once confided in me. It was different times. Margaret had been miserable all her life. She'd felt chained to a man she did not love. Trapped with only one way out. But to make her last words an accusation? My heart aches for Edith. What a burden she must have carried all these years.

"I thought she blamed me. For everything." Tears run down Edith's cheeks. I pat her back.

Most of what I know about Margaret, Henry has told me. He'd loved his wife deeply, though she never returned the feeling. To him, she'd been a bird with broken wings. He'd cared for her, tried to make her happy. But the darkness in her soul had eclipsed all joy. He'd told me about the bottles of pills he found after her death. All untouched. She hadn't taken her prescription drugs in over a year.

"Margaret was sick," I say, not sure myself if I am referring to her depression or her suicide note.

Edith shakes her head and wipes away the tears with my handkerchief. She is still staring at the corner. I squint to see what she is looking at. There's nothing but darkness.

"The night I left you, I saw it too. The shadow. I finally understood what she meant. The note was a warning."

She falls silent. I am suddenly afraid. It takes me a while to summon up the courage to ask her. "What happened to our child?"

She stares at her hands, which are folded as if in prayer. The knuckles are white because she presses them so tightly together. "I was stupid. Thought there might be a chance to make it go away. That's what I did. Make it go away."

A sudden wave of grief takes hold of me, para-lyzing my heart. Anger shocks it to beating again. It had been my child too. The urge to yell at her becomes overwhelming. I take a few breaths to get back control and realize I'm not the one suffering most. She had wanted that child even more. I gently stroke her back. "It's okay," I say, ignoring my bleeding heart.

Edith just sits there. "Nothing's okay," she whispers. "It's still there."

"The child?"

She shakes her head, her eyes fixated on the dark corner. "Did you know I'm named after my grandmother?" Edith laughs. It sounds desperate. "She hanged herself after my mother was born."

Edith tears her gaze away from the dreadful corner and looks at me. Her eyes are expanded.

"I'm to be its next prey."

The acceptance in her voice scares me most. I clasp her folded hands and hold her gaze while I rub some warmth into her icy fingers. I want to tell her those kinds of shadows do not exist. The ones that hunt people down. Her eyes make the words stick in my throat. They are black because the pupils are dilated so much. Trapped inside this blackness is a fragile child afraid of the dark. It hits me like a gut punch when I realize Haimi is right. Edith's death is imminent. Edith believes the shadow to be real. It will kill her, no matter what I believe.

A janitor opens the door and drags a garbage bag to the trash cans. Edith withdraws her hands, gets up, and brushes off her skirt. "Well, I'm not your problem. Not anymore."

She does not look at me. Her guard is up again, our connection lost. She gives me back my handkerchief. "Thanks for listening. I hope one day you can forgive me. For everything."

She wants to leave, but I hold her back. "I'll protect you. There's still hope."

Edith smiles at me. It's one of those smiles meant for people who have yet to come to terms with the facts of life.

Before she steps through the door, she says without looking back, "I don't even know why I let that mutt win. It was like my heart was drumming its name and I had to dance to the beat."

The door falls shut behind her, and its sound shakes me to action. I have a life to save.

I hasten back to the arena. The announcer is already telling people to head to their seats. The final event is to begin in ten minutes. I make my way through hundreds of eager dog lovers and spectators who trot through the benching area to their seats. I need to talk to Lady Winthrop before I step into that ring.

Cynthia is exactly where I expect her to be, behind the purple curtain that veils the backstage area from the ring, giving last instructions to the finalists' handlers. She is leading Harvey, who handles Irving himself, to the front of the line.

"Winner of working group enters first," she says when I tap on her shoulder.

"We need to talk."

Harvey looks at me intently.

"In private," I urge.

Cynthia glares at me. "Where the hell have you been?" she hisses.

I grab her elbow and drag her with me. "Sorry, but this is important. I need you to buy me some time."

"Are you out of your mind? We are on a schedule." Her face is red with anger. My feelings must be written all over my face, because when she sees my expression, she looks worried. "What's wrong?" she asks.

"Edith. Just give me fifteen minutes, that's all I ask. You said you owed me one."

Cynthia sighs and clenches her jaw. "Are you going to tell me what's up?"

"Later. Promise. First, I need to find Lady Winthrop." I turn and head toward the benching stations where I saw her last.

"She won't be back there!" Cynthia calls after me. She hands the clipboard to her assistant, whispers something in her ear, and runs toward me.

"I'll get you to her," she says.

I look at her in surprise.

"She'll be in the VIP lounge. She always watches the show from there."

I follow her.

"How would you know where Lady Winthrop is?" I ask.

"She's the personal reason I can't judge today. Also known as my mom."

I open my mouth to reply something, but Cynthia glares at me. "No comments, please!" We hasten through the arena side by side. "You'd better fill me in before we get there."

"You won't believe it anyway."

"Try me," she says. So I do.

In the end, it is Cynthia who does the convincing, not me. I pace up and down outside the door, playing out all the options in my head.

"That was fun. We should do that more often, Mother." Cynthia leaves the VIP lounge with a cheerful gleam in her eye.

Lady Winthrop, who shows her out, is neatly dressed in an expensive Chanel suit, her hair in an accurate bun. She looks more like an embodiment of Cynthia's opposite than her mother.

"You agree?" I ask.

Lady Winthrop looks down her nose at me. She gives the convincing expression of someone recently been forced to swallow a toad. "I'd hardly call blackmail an agreement."

"History is going to be written today, Mother. Better make it the Westminster way. Wouldn't you agree?"

Lady Winthrop purses her lips. "It's me who pays the price."

"It's also you taking the prize," Cynthia says. The lady turns without another word.

Today

I see the boy run away. I paid him a buck to ring the bell. Nobody opens the door. The box begins to wiggle. I don't take my eyes off it.

"How long do we wait?" I shift around on my car seat. I've grown attached to Hope the last couple of weeks. I don't want her to fall into the wrong hands.

"Have a little patience," says Haimi's soft voice from the back seat of the car. She puts her tiny hand on my shoulder and gives me a slight squeeze. "Thanks for joining our path," she adds.

"I have to pass the time between now and my future somehow. Why not help save some lives?"

I smile at her through the rearview mirror. In her lap, the pup is still asleep. Although Irving is adorable with his oversized head and the way he snores melts my heart, the sight of him stings. I miss the old mongrel. Who'd have thought? Certainly not me. It has been hard to watch him die.

Not dead, the familiar voice inside my head sounds sleepy, *moved on. But thanks for missing the old me.* Irving is awake now. He yawns and sticks out his tiny pink tongue. I feel like yawning too. It has been a long day. It took forever to drive here.

From the corner of my eye, I notice a movement. Finally, the door opens. Edith steps out and looks around, confused. She notices the box. She bends down and fumbles with the knot. As soon as she has it open, Hope's big head pops up, the lid wobbling on it.

I get all tense.

"You're sure she's a shadow hunter?"

Now it is up to the Hunts to roll their eyes at me. "We're sure," they say in unison.

Edith takes Hope out of the box. She holds the pup with stretched arms and looks at it from all sides. Hope's appearance might be an acquired taste, but she's by far the cutest of the litter and takes mostly after her mother, the four-time Westminster winner. The fur on her body is silky smooth and has white-brown spots. On her head, the hair is black and wiry and sticks out in all directions. It looks as if she's wearing a wig for fun. Edith's face lights up when she looks into the pup's eyes. Hope's are mostly brown, speckled with amber dots. All Eppingers have mesmerizing eyes. But that's not the only thing that makes them special.

"When is it going to happen?" I ask, tapping on the wheel. *You've waited four months for this. You can certainly wait a moment longer,* Irving's growling voice sounds in my head. Irving stands on Haimi's lap, his front paws pushed against the window, his little hind legs shaking from the strain of standing upright. He doesn't take his eyes off his little sister. Or is Hope his daughter? I shake my head. It does not matter *what* she is. It only matters *that* she is.

Edith hugs the pup. The moment her ear reaches Hope's muzzle, the little dog snaps at something invisible. Hope gives the thing a serious churn and only stops when Edith grabs her at the nape.

She laughs and shakes her head. She has already fallen for the dog. Who wouldn't?

"Is it dead now?" I am referring to the shadow.

Harvey wipes the drool off his mouth before he answers. "Hope's not strong enough to kill it yet. She needs to grow up first." He yawns. "Mission one completed. Let's find a motel and rest for a few hours. Tomorrow, it's time to set out on missions two, three, and four." He lowers his gaze. On his lap is another box in which three pups sleep cuddled against each other.

"Maybe it's time to call them by their names. They must be on there somewhere." I nod at Harvey's skin.

He shrugs and pets the brown puppy that will save a little boy from drowning seven years from now.

"They are." Haimi giggles. "Harvey's a prophecy, after all. But I'm the only one who can read him, and I never tell it all. Spoils the surprise."

I am so used to the Hunts' antics by now that I don't even think twice about the absurdity of Haimi's remark. My thoughts are with Edith and Hope anyway. I am not ready to leave them. Not yet.

"What will happen until Hope's fully grown?"

"Guess she'll have a ball chasing the shadow around," Harvey says. "Don't worry, it won't have a chance to hurt her again. And once Hope catches it for good, a new chapter in your lives begins."

"Sure?"

He winks at me and taps with a finger to the spot near his left nipple, where Edith's and my story is written. "Dead sure. Even had it branded."

I laugh and start the car.

As I stop at the crossroad, I have a last glance at Edith through the rearview mirror. She has discovered the note I attached to Hope's name tag. I mouth the words as she reads them:

Now, you'll always have Hope. Keep her close.

She's special. I've made sure.

I didn't leave my name. She'll know who it's from. She has a dozen love letters in the same hand.

As I turn the corner, I wonder what making love to her will feel like after all those years. Memories of past encounters flash in front of my inner eye. I wind down the window for cool air, when a sudden realization startles me. With burning ears and squinted eyes, I watch Irving through the rearview mirror. He looks out of the window, all innocence, but I swear he's grinning.

You Care? Please Share!

Did you like this story? Then please consider leaving a review. As an independent author, reviews are one of the most important ways I have to get the word out. Your review will encourage others to grab the book. Thank you!

www.ingramcontent.com/pod-product-compliance
Lightning Source LLC
LaVergne TN
LVHW031436170726
843492LV00010B/3026